GODDARD

This edition is only available for sale in school book clubs and school book fairs.

Special thanks to Manny Galan
Pencils by Kelsey Shannon

SIMON SPOTLIGHT
An imprint of Simon & Schuster Children's Publishing Division
1230 Avenue of the Americas, New York, New York 10020
Copyright © 2001 Paramount Pictures and Viacom International Inc. All rights reserved.
NICKELODEON, *Jimmy Neutron Boy Genius,* and all related titles, logos, and characters
are trademarks of Viacom International Inc.
All rights reserved, including the right of reproduction in whole or in part in any form.
SIMON SPOTLIGHT and colophon are registered trademarks of Simon & Schuster.
Manufactured in the United States of America
First Edition 10 9 8 7 6 5 4 3 2 1
ISBN 0-689-85016-6

JIMMY NEUTRON
BOY GENIUS

by Terry Collins

illustrated by Patrick Spaziante

SIMON SPOTLIGHT/NICKELODEON

New York   London   Toronto   Sydney   Singapore

Jimmy Neutron barrel-rolled
his rocket into an upright position.

"Engaging pulse rockets!" he announced.
"Launch the satellite, Carl!"

Carl blinked. "Uh, what do I do again?"

"You're the deployment system, Carl. You just . . .
throw it!"

Carl hauled back and threw, but the satellite landed
back in his lap.

"Quick!" Jimmy yelled. "Give me your lunch!"

Jimmy grabbed a can of soda from Carl's lunch box and
shook it hard. Then he attached it to the satellite, popped
the tab, and . . . *WHOOSH!* The satellite shot up and
spun into orbit.

Jimmy high-fived Carl. "Don't try *that* at home!"

Moments later a loud crash startled Jimmy's parents.

"James Isaac Neutron!" Jimmy's mom yelled. "What do you think you're doing up there?"

"Just launching a communication satellite," Jimmy replied. "I'm on the verge of making contact with an advanced alien civilization!"

"Aliens!" his mom cried. "We've warned you not to talk to strangers!" she scolded. "You're grounded!"

"Pukin' Pluto!" Jimmy said to his robotic dog, Goddard. "How could Mom ground me on the night of the grand opening of Retroland?"

Goddard's mechanical ears perked up and his computer screen flipped open.

"Sneak out?" Jimmy read.

"Bark! Bark!" Goddard replied.

Jimmy scratched his head. But how do I get past Mom and Dad? he wondered.

"I've got it!" Jimmy cried. "I'll use my Neutron Shrink Ray 2.0!"

He pulled the gadget out of his dresser drawer and made a few adjustments with his Retro-Wrench.

ZAP! Jimmy shrunk himself down to the size of an action figure, then strolled right past his parents and out the front door.

Then Jimmy zapped himself back to normal size and raced to Retroland to meet his friends.

"Wow, it's even better than the commercial," Carl sighed.

Jimmy threw his arms over his friends' shoulders. "Gentlemen," he said, "this will be a night we shan't easily forget."

First the boys glided over Retroland in the cloud-scraping Eye in the Sky cable-car ride.

Once back on ground they headed for the Lose Your Lunch ride, followed by the head-twisting Pain in the Neck ride.

"Hey, look!" said Carl. "A shooting star!"

"You get to make a wish," said Sheen.

Jimmy grinned. "I know what *I'd* wish for. I'd wish for no more parents. That way we could do *whatever* we wanted!"

Across town a single spaceship appeared in the night sky. Then two. Then dozens upon dozens, all of them hovering over the homes of Retroville.

Within minutes every grown-up in town was enveloped in an eerie green light . . . and sucked into the spacecrafts!

HI! MY NAME IS JIMMY NEUTRON AND THESE ARE MY PARENTS. . . .

Onboard the command ship a Yokian alien translated Jimmy's satellite. "The large humans look edible," the commander squawked. "Send word to His Royal Majesty! The search is over!" The first officer activated the tractor beams.

The next morning Jimmy found his house empty except for a strange note.
Outside kids were everywhere comparing the same notes.

"D-D-Did they *all* go to Florida?" Carl stammered.

No parents? Jimmy mused. Could his wish really have come true?

"Goddard," he said, "scan for adult life-forms."

Goddard's computer screen beeped and blinked. There were no grown-ups anywhere within radar range!

Cindy Vortex was sitting with her best friend, Libby, at a table nearby. "What's the deal with the missing grown-ups, Neutron?" she asked. "Any theories?"

"They took a vacation," Jimmy replied. "Didn't you get the note?"

Cindy rolled her eyes. "We *all* got the note, genius."

Something is wrong, Jimmy thought. Why would my parents go on vacation without telling me? And why would *all* of our parents go to Florida at the same time?

Jimmy brought his note to his secret laboratory and fed it through his handwriting-analysis machine.

"Just as I suspected, Goddard," he said. "This note's a fake!"

Goddard barked, drawing Jimmy's attention to a blinking red light.

"Jumpin' Jupiter! The long-range Space Scanner has detected something!" Jimmy cried. "Goddard, the Earth's been visited by aliens!"

The kids of Retroville gathered in Jimmy's backyard.

"Why did you want us to come here, Neutron?" Cindy demanded.

Jimmy addressed the restless crowd. "An unknown alien race has abducted our parents! And it's our job to get them back! Now, who's with me?"

First there was silence. Then a loud cheer erupted.

Work began immediately as Jimmy and his friends prepared for the journey into space.

"Where are we going to find a space fleet, huh, boy genius?" Cindy said, smirking.

Jimmy peered out at Retroland. "Luckily, the mechanical minds of most modern amusement park rides lend themselves to reprogramming."

Within hours the space fleet was ready for takeoff.

"Goddard," Jimmy commanded, "initiate flight sequence!"

The Retroville fleet was light-years away from home as they followed the ion trail left behind by the alien ships. But the trail led right through a meteor shower.

"Holy Moon Pie!" Jimmy cried. "Evasive action, everybody!"

The rockets zigged and zagged to avoid being smashed to pieces.

"My butterfly smells funny,"
Carl said as the rocket's engine
overheated from the quick maneuvers.
Once past the meteors a great green
planet loomed ahead . . . planet Yolkus.

After landing on planet Yolkus, Jimmy led a search party to investigate.

"They've evolved beyond the need for mere conventional bodies!" Jimmy marveled as the group creeped into the Royal Yokian Palace. "They must be millions of years ahead of us!"

"You mean they evolved into . . . snot?" Cindy asked.

"Eeaauuu." Libby wrinkled her nose.

"Shhh!" Jimmy whispered, pointing at their parents.

"What are those goofy-looking things on their heads?" Cindy asked.

Jimmy looked grim. "Mind-control beanies," he said. "Our parents are like helpless puppets!"

"Oh, Ooblar. These humans look so scrawny," King Goobot said as he inspected the catch. "And they don't look very appetizing."

"No, no, Poultra will be pleased," assured Ooblar. "Goody! I just hope they shriek when eaten," the king replied mischievously. "I do so love it when our sacrifices scream!"

Just as the rescue attempt was about to begin, the search party was surrounded by Yokian guards.

"Don't look so surprised!" King Goobot gloated. "We *are* an advanced alien race. Now you'll get to watch your parents be sacrificed to the mighty Poultra!"

Jimmy's eyes narrowed. "My mom and dad are *not* snack treats!"

"I beg to differ, Mr. Neutron. And after all it was your silly, little satellite that directed us to your puny planet in the first place!" the king said, sneering. "Guards! Throw these scrawny vermin into the dungeon until they are of worthier size!"

"Nice job, Neutron!" Cindy said. "How are you going to get us out of this mess?"

Jimmy spotted Libby's mobile phone. "Let me see that," he said. "I know who can help, *if* he's within range . . ."

From outside the locked door they heard a faint bark.

"Goddard!" Jimmy called out. "Play dead!"

BOOM! A loud explosion rocked the dungeon, blowing through the cell door. As the smoke cleared, pieces of Goddard were scattered everywhere.

"Oh, no!" Carl cried. "D-D-Did he self-destruct?"

"Not exactly," Jimmy replied as the robotic dog pieced himself back together. "Good boy, Goddard!"

The Yokians had all gathered in the coliseum for the festival. "Beekaw! Beekaw! Beekaw!" they chanted as Poultra broke free of his giant egg. The parents stood motionless, paralyzed by their mind-control beanies.

Jimmy snuck into the control tower. "Time for your break!" he said, and he cracked the shell of the Yokian controller with a karate chop. He grabbed the mind-control joystick and jerked it. And the parents moved right through the exit!

"W-W-What?!" cried King Goobot. Then he noticed Jimmy. "Neutron!" he said in disbelief. "Do something, Ooblar. They're getting away!"

Just then Poultra loomed overhead. He looked hungry. And he was looking right at King Goobot and Ooblar!

"D-D-Don't worry, Poultra," said the king. "We'll get your dinner back."

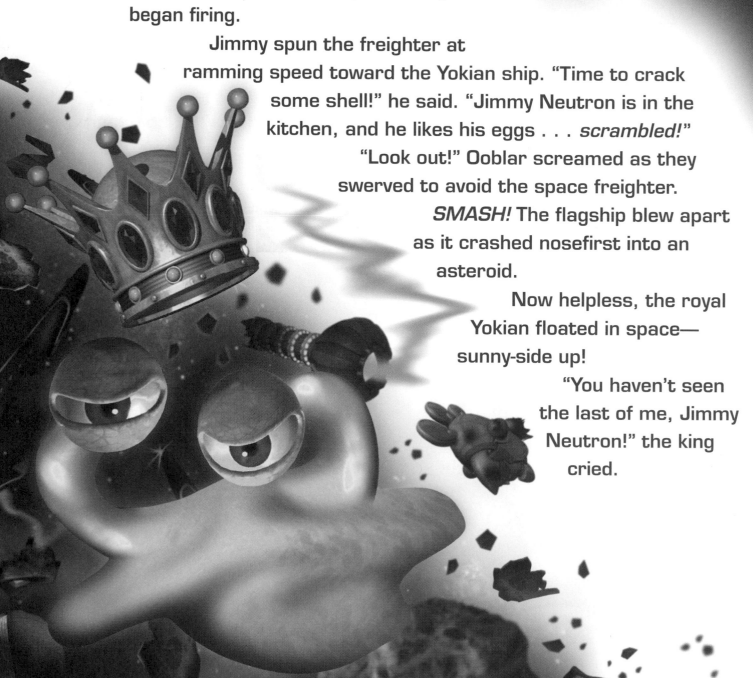

With Jimmy at the helm, the citizens of Retroville blasted back toward Earth in a Yokian space freighter.

But King Goobot and Ooblar weren't going to let them escape so easily. At the controls of the royal flagship, the king began firing.

Jimmy spun the freighter at ramming speed toward the Yokian ship. "Time to crack some shell!" he said. "Jimmy Neutron is in the kitchen, and he likes his eggs . . . *scrambled!*"

"Look out!" Ooblar screamed as they swerved to avoid the space freighter.

SMASH! The flagship blew apart as it crashed nosefirst into an asteroid.

Now helpless, the royal Yokian floated in space—sunny-side up!

"You haven't seen the last of me, Jimmy Neutron!" the king cried.

Soon everything was back to normal in Retroville.

"There you go, gentlemen," Mrs. Neutron said as she placed breakfast on the kitchen table. "Fried eggs, just the way you like them."

"Thanks, Mom," Jimmy replied weakly.

"Remember, you promised to mow the lawn today, Jimmy," Mrs. Neutron added as she left the room.

Carl pushed his plate away, disgusted. "So, uh, did you really destroy all those mind-control beanies?" he asked.

"Yeah," Jimmy replied, glancing out the window at his dad. "Well, I kept one . . . for research, you know. Strictly for research!"

GODDARD